# Blueberries for Sal

Also by Robert McCloskey

# Blueberries for Sal

## BY ROBERT McCLOSKEY

SCHOLASTIC INC.

New York   Toronto   London   Auckland   Sydney

ISBN 0-590-40923-9

Copyright © 1948 by Robert McCloskey. Copyright © renewed by Robert McCloskey, 1976.  All rights reserved. Published by Scholastic Inc.,
730 Broadway, New York, NY 10003,
by arrangement with Viking Penguin, Inc.

70  69  68  67  66  65  64  63  62                                                                                          12  13  14  15/0

Printed in the U.S.A.                                                                08
First Scholastic printing, March 1987

# Blueberries for Sal

ONE day, Little Sal went with her mother to Blueberry Hill to pick blueberries.

Little Sal brought along her small tin pail and her mother brought her large tin pail to put berries in. "We will take our berries home and can them," said her mother. "Then we will have food for the winter."

Little Sal picked three berries and dropped them in her little tin pail . . . *kuplink, kuplank, kuplunk!*

She picked three more berries and ate them. Then she
picked more berries and dropped one in the pail—*kuplunk!*
And the rest she ate. Then Little Sal ate all four blueberries out of her pail!

Her mother walked slowly through the bushes, picking blueberries as she went and putting them in her pail. Little Sal struggled along behind, picking blueberries and eating every single one.

Little Sal hurried ahead and dropped a blueberry in her mother's pail. It didn't sound *kuplink!* because the bottom of the pail was already covered with berries. She reached down inside to get her berry back. Though she really didn't mean to, she pulled out a large handful, because there were so many blueberries right up close to the one she had put in.

Her mother stopped picking and said, "Now, Sal, you run along and pick your own berries. Mother wants to take her berries home and can them for next winter."

Her mother went back to her picking, but Little Sal, because her feet were tired of standing and walking, sat down in the middle of a large clump of bushes and ate blueberries.

On the other side of Blueberry Hill, Little Bear came with his mother to eat blueberries.

"Little Bear," she said, "eat lots of berries and grow big and fat. We must store up food for the long, cold winter."

Little Bear followed behind his mother as she walked slowly through the bushes eating berries. Little Bear stopped now and then to eat berries.

Then he had to hustle along to catch up!

Because his feet were tired of hustling, he picked out
a large clump of bushes and sat down right in the middle
and ate blueberries.

24

Over on the other side of the hill, Little Sal ate all of the berries she could reach from where she was sitting, then she started out to find her mother.

She heard a noise from around a rock and thought,
"That is my mother walking along!"

28

But it was a mother crow and her children, and they stopped eating berries and flew away, saying, "Caw, Caw, Caw." Then she heard another noise in the bushes and thought, "That is *surely* my mother and I will go that way."

But it was Little Bear's mother instead. She was tramping along, eating berries, and thinking about storing up food for the winter. Little Sal tramped right along behind.

By this time, Little Bear had eaten all the berries he could reach without moving from his clump of bushes. Then he hustled off to catch up with his mother. He hunted and hunted but his mother was nowhere to be seen. He heard a noise from over a stump and thought, "That is my mother walking along."

But it was a mother partridge and her children. They stopped eating berries and hurried away. Then he heard a noise in the bushes and thought, "That is surely *my* mother. I will hustle that way!"

But it was Little Sal's mother instead! She was walking along, picking berries, and thinking about canning them for next winter. Little Bear hustled right along behind.

Little Bear and Little Sal's mother and Little Sal and Little Bear's mother were all mixed up with each other among the blueberries on Blueberry Hill.

39

Little Bear's mother heard Sal walking along behind and thought it was Little Bear and she said, "Little Bear," *munch, munch*, "Eat all you —" *gulp*, "can possibly hold!" *swallow*. Little Sal said nothing. She picked three berries and dropped them, *kuplink, kuplank, kuplunk*, in her small tin pail.

Little Bear's mother turned around to see what on earth could make a noise like *kuplunk!*

*"Garumpf!"* she cried, choking on a mouthful of berries, "This is not my child! Where is Little Bear?" She took one good look and backed away. (She was old enough to be shy of people, even a very small person like Little Sal.) Then she turned around and walked off very fast to hunt for Little Bear.

Little Sal's mother heard Little Bear tramping along behind and thought it was Little Sal. She kept right on picking and thinking about canning blueberries for next winter.

Little Bear padded up and peeked into her pail. Of course, he only wanted to taste a *few* of what was inside, but there were so many and they were so close together, that he tasted a Tremendous Mouthful by mistake. "Now, Sal," said Little Sal's mother without turning around, "you run along and pick your own berries. Mother wants to can these for next winter." Little Bear tasted another Tremendous Mouthful, and almost spilled the entire pail of blueberries!

Little Sal's mother turned around and gasped, "My Goodness, *you* are not Little Sal! Where, oh where, is my child?"

Little Bear just sat munching and munching and swallowing and licking his lips.

Little Sal's mother slowly backed away. (She was old enough to be shy of bears, even very small bears like Little Bear.) Then she turned and walked away quickly to look for Little Sal.

She hadn't gone very far before she heard a *kuplink!*
*kuplank! kuplunk!*

She knew just what made that kind of a noise!

Little Bear's mother had not hunted very long before she heard a hustling sound that stopped now and then to munch and swallow. She knew just what made that kind of a noise.

Little Bear and his mother went home down one side
of Blueberry Hill, eating blueberries all the way, and full
of food stored up for next winter.

And Little Sal and her mother went down the other side of Blueberry Hill, picking berries all the way, and drove home with food to can for next winter — a whole pail of blueberries and three more besides.